CAPtuRED THE NIPPLE KILLER

ROBERT LEWIS BARROS M.D.

CAPtuRED
THE NIPPLE KILLER

A NOVEL

BY

ROBERT L. BARROS, M.D

CITIOFBOOKS, INC.
3736 Eubank NE Suite A1
Albuquerque, NM 87111-3579
www.citiofbooks.com
Hotline: 1 (877) 389-2759
Fax: 1 (505) 930-7244

Ordering Information:
Quantity sales. Special discounts are available on quantity purchases by corporations, associations, and others. For details, contact the publisher at the address above.

Printed in the United States of America.
ISBN-13:   Paperback   979-8-89391-253-1
               eBook   979-8-89391-255-5
               Hardback   979-8-89391-254-8

Library of Congress Control Number: 2024916680

It was the most famous case ever in Seco. Usually a peaceful community, where everybody knows each other. Now, there is total cayuse in town. There is no place to park, especially near the courthouse. Cameras everywhere. The TVs in the whole country, all tuned in to hear about the nipple killer. It took more than four years to finally capture this evil man, after he killed so many of our woman.

He frightened us. There was no peace in town. We were afraid to leave our homes. Now we can go to the park and listen to the birds. The kids can go back to their T-ball league. The bars and the restaurants are open, as usual. Peace finely arrived in Seco unless we were around the courthouse.

Outside the courthouse, it is cause, because people are lined up trying to go inside. Crowds outside, just to get a glimpse of the nipple killer. All the press are outside waiting to capture the images and get information about what is going on. They all wanted to know all about him. We are finally getting some information about this evil man.

The people in the media try to interview him as he passes by. Everybody is saying, we have heard so many things, but we don't know if it really is fact or just gossip. We all wanted to know why they call him the nipple killer.

Everybody that sees him says he does not look like a killer. He looks like a good-looking regular guy.

Not much information had been given to the press, except the information they had to share at the time he was captured, and the limited information after every crime he committed. The police, and investigators started calling him the nipple killer, but they hadn't told us why. So, we call him the nipple killer too, that is the name the police and the investigators have given him. We are now beginning to understand why.

Inside the court, they are arguing about procedure, jurors, admissible evidence, dates and he is laughing watching them all. I guess I must be very important to have every eye in America watching me he thought. They all want to know what I did, and why they called me the nipple killer. I have always known that I am very good looking. When the guards come to get me to be present in court, I want to be well shaven, and my hair perfectly combed, it is my right. When I am in front of the cameras, I pose for them, and I give them a big friendly innocent smile. Most of the people that come out to see me are women. I wink at them, and smile. They appear confused, little do they know how I would love to get my hands on them.

They have me in a holding cell near the court; from there I can hear and see the TV on top of the detective's desk. I used to run this whole department. Some of these guys worked for me for years and were my good friends when I was the chief of police here. Now, occasionally some of them come and talk to me. They want to know about the nipples. I always tell them that my attorney has told me not to discuss any aspect of the case with anyone.

Occasionally when one of them comes to talk to me, I ask him to turn the TV so I can watch it and be able to hear it from my cell. The new chief of police said it would be OK. Because he is new, he has more tolerance. I guess some treat me like a celebrity, but most of them hate me with all their guts. They trusted me, and I was the criminal.

When they first caught me, the FBI made me show them every detail, where the crimes were committed, and how, and where I abducted my victims.

They have all the evidence. The nipples, the tongue, the marijuana bag, the shirt, the DNA of all the victims.

At first, I played their game. I re-enacted all my crimes. I turned over all the evidence. Then my heart turned evil. I thought, I did all that, so what?

I was always distracted in court. I went along with my attorney's advice. They wanted me to plead not guilty. Day after day, the court goes on. When one of the members of the jury looks at me, I look back at him like I am going to eat him. I can tell they are frightened by me. I am sure they are thinking we better put this guy away, because if he gets out, he will come looking for me.

I played the tuff guy role in court. I didn't care. So what I said to myself, I don't give a dam. Nothing matters to me anymore. All I know is that I am famous. Everybody wants to know what I did, and who I am.

Finely, the jury found me guilty, and the judge gave me the death sentence. Of course this is subject to appeals, and my execution date has not been determined.

They moved me out of the holding cell and took me to a maximum-security prison. Every time we went out into the yard, the inmates would jump at me and give me a beating. I hurt every day. They would hit me so hard, I often passed out, and then they would leave me on the ground.

The guards didn't like me eider. They felt betrayed. The chief of police was the criminal. So, when I would get a beating, though I hurt, I didn't know whether to go to the infirmary with the grads, or make it back into my cell, to the block where they have all the condemned prisoners waiting to be executed, DEATH ROW. They are now keeping me isolated. They are afraid that they will try to kill me.

I have learned so much. Every day I walked into my cell in pain. Day after day, they torture not only my body but totally disconnected and shattered my Mind. I could not have a rational thought. I was really in my limit. I wanted to kill myself; I wanted to die.

I had so much time in my cell. I really wanted to end it all. I asked if I could have something to read. They brought me newspapers, magazines, and books. The Chaplin came by every day, as the months went by. I never paid attention to him. I always just ignored him. One day he invited me to meet with a group of inmates that were waiting execution. He said that they talked about their problems, and what is in their minds, and in their hearts, and they find the power of prayer. I had no interest in any of that, but it gave me something else to spend my time.

They also required that I meet with the psychologist five times a week. I could not have a rational thought at first, I thought she was wasting her time, but she knew her business well. She finely got me to talk, and after years of daily therapy, I began to unravel and unload all this heavy weight of hate, and rage, that I had been carrying all my life. Hate and evil was in me, and that dictated my life, to the point that I felt it was my right to kill, torture, and let my sexual rage out. This was imbedded in me and guided my life since I was a child. I really didn't know right from wrong in my life. Though I knew the law, and was willing to enforce it in other people, I thought it did not apply to me. All I knew was that if it made me feel good no matter how evil, it was OK. I was the only one that mattered.

After years of therapy sessions with Dr. White, and the great effort by the Chaplin Divine, I discovered how wrong I had been. I began to feel ashamed. Sorrow went into me, and the faces of all my victims, when they begged for their lives, began to hunt me. I discovered I needed to die. Every day is now torture.

I have been here waiting for my execution for six years. My attorney, Mr. Raines, thinks that all this that happened in my life is not my fault. He argues to the court that I have been a victim of child abuse, and neglect, and that is really the reason I have reacted this way. I tell the Judge that I deserve to die. My life is over. I understand now that it was not my right to kill, just because I it gave me pleasure. I now finely understand that these people I killed had the right to live, and it was not my right to kill them.

Mr. Raines wants the judge to give me life in prison, with the possibility to be rehabilitated, and be out on parole. I can't live the rest of my life in prison. I now understand what I have done. I can't face my wife or children. I don't accept their visits. I know it was a mistake that I was born. Every time I go before a judge, I tell them I deserve to die, and I want to die. I ask them to execute me right away. Unfortunately, this gives the judge doubt about my execution. Everyone that is on death row, asks not to be executed, so that confuses them, and they are afraid of making the wrong decision. They keep postponing my execution.

I have confessed to all my crimes. I have shown them where I committed them. They have been able to identify the victims with DNA from the nipples. They know it all. I even told them about the needless killings I did when I was in the military. I told them how I killed my grandfather when I was just a boy. They have no doubt that I am evil, and I am the one that committed these horrific crimes. Still here I am six years after they condemn me to death.

I stay here in prison with the guilt that tortures my brain every minute I am awake, I am ashamed of my evil pass. There is nowhere to hide. I need to shut off the images that cross my mind every second of every minute, of every day. It won't stop. I hear the voices of my victims pleading for their lives. Their lives wasted for my evil pleasure. The feeling that all that mattered was to satisfy my pleasure, and hidden anger and rage. I felt inside my head that I deserved to do this, and that gave me permission to do this evil, malignant, and brutal behavior that gave me intense pleasure manifested by sexual rage, and blood thirst. A subconscious revenge. Someone had to pay. It was my job to make sure someone paid.

I did not understand it. It took me years to finally discover the evil that was in me. I say "was" because it is all gone from me now. All that is left, is the sounds of my victims that never stop ripping through my brain and shame my heart. I don't know where to hide. They don't understand. I need to shut these sounds off. I need to die. I need to have peace.

I WAS BORN WITH THE DEVIL IN ME. My name is Richard; I am waiting in death row for my execution. This is my story.

I was born to an alcoholic, and drug attic mother. I had Alcoholic Fetal Syndrome, which affected my development and growth.

Since I can remember, I had hatred and anger in me. There was something in me that gave me joy and pleasure seeing people and animals suffer. This was my only pleasure.

I was slower than the other kids, at least at first. My development was taking more time than normal. My brain had been poorly programed, I guess. Early on, I was weak, it took me three or four years to be able to stand and walk. I don't know if this was as a result of alcoholic fetal syndrome, or neglect from my parents.

I had absolutely no one I could count on, there was no one I could trust. No one guided me, so I followed my heart, and my heart was evil. From the time I was little, I wanted to break things, make people angry, and fight, and become violent. I felt at home when there was hatred and violence. No one liked me. I was a loaner. Sure, my auntie Julie, my dad's sister, would come to visit, and she would always ask, where is Ricki? The next thing she asked was, where is the beer? She was an alcoholic, like my mother and father. They were in their elements, getting drunk and stoned together. When I came down to have breakfast in the morning, they were all passed out on the floor. I'd go into the kitchen, and the refrigerator was empty, all there was in the kitchen was about a hundred empty cans of beer.

I didn't get along with my neighbors, they all thought I was troubled. When there was no food in the house, I would watch to see if my neighbors were gone. When they were gone, I would go through the backyard into their house. I'd go through their things, and take food from the refrigerator, and see if I could find some money. I even stole a gun from them.

When I was eight, they sent me to live with my grandfather. He was kind but strict. He tried to teach me the right way to go. He would take me to church every Sunday, and he tried to teach me to be honest and kind. I hated him. He tried to be good to me. He would take me to school and pick me up every day. We often went for ice cream after school. I could see he really loved me.

One day, I took a chicken from the barn, grabbed it by the neck, and took it outside. I chopped off her head with a machete. I loved to see blood spurting all over the place. The chicken ran around for a few seconds without her head, squirting blood. My Grandfather cried all morning when he saw me kill the chicken. He watched my laughter and joy. He saw me do it from the window of the house upstairs. He could not control me. He punished me, he told me I had to stay in my room all day.

He went to the store to get some groceries. He had a big freezer in the second floor of the barn. It was like a loft that had a rail on the end. He kept the frozen food there. He bought a lot of frozen food because he didn't like to cook.

The tractor was in the barn below. My grandfather had been

plowing all morning and brought the tractor into the barn. It had sharp round plowing disks. I waited for him on the second floor of the barn. When he arrived, he went into the kitchen to make himself a sandwich. He then started emptying the grocery bags that were in the truck into these boxes, which he then brought up to the barn with all the frozen food. He only went to the market once a month, and he had a lot of frozen food. That's why he needed this gigantic freezer. He started going up the stairs with the frozen food.

I had been thinking if I should do this or not. I wanted to do it. I hated him. When he came up, I waited until he was close to the rail, and I pushed him hard from behind. He went over the rail, and he landed on top of the tractor. The round blades on the tractor made deep cuts on his head. He was bleeding severely. In my mind I was saying: that is what you deserve. The fall had cut him on the side of the head, and had opened an artery, and the blood was spurting from the side of his head. It made me feel good to see the blood spurting out of him. He pleaded for his life as he laid their bleeding. He begged me to call 911 for help. I waited until all the blood had gone out of him, and he was dead, then I called 911. I told them that I had just walked into the barn and found my grandfather on top of the tractor. I told them that I was afraid to move him, so I called 911.

After that, I had to move back with my parents.

My Mom had been brought up by my grandparents. They gave her everything. My Grandparents had inherited the farm from my grandmother's parents. They lived a simple life, but they had lots of money and property. They were good, hard working religious people. When I was living with my grandfather, he would tell me all the history of the family. He was very sad to have lost my grandmother at an early age. He told me she was a chain smoker, and he could not convince her to stop. She was exceptionally beautiful, and she thought it was fashionable to smoke. He would imitate how she would hold her cigarette and blow out the smoke.

He told me how they had spoiled my mother. She was an only child. She was very beautiful and graceful; my grandfather told me. My mother had blond hair and brown eyes. She was always the best in her class. She was focused on whatever undertaking she took. She loved to read. Her grandparents adored her. Like her parents, they spoiled her too.

One day, she had a very high fever and was vomiting repeatedly. They took her to the Emergency Room. She was then taken to pediatric ICU where they discovered she had meningitis. They didn't know if she would recover. Her parents, and her Grandparents were devastated. They were religious people and prayed on their knees for her every day. Though the doctors told them she had very little chance of survival, she made it though. That made her even more precious to the family. They over protected her, and they let her do whatever she wanted. She was a good girl until she got into High school, and she got into the wrong crowd.

My grandparents always trusted her. My Mom became an alcoholic at a very early age, but grandparents never knew it. When she was sixteen, they bought her a brand-new red mustang convertible. They trusted her when she told them that she was going to spend the weekend with her best friend, but she would go to her boyfriend's apartment instead. He was ten years older than her. When my mom got pregnant, she broke my grandmother's heart, but my mom didn't care. In high school, all the girls admired her because she had this good-looking older guy and had this beautiful red convertible. They all covered for her. She would go with her boyfriend to these wild parties where they all got drunk and stoned. At first it was only on the weekends, but then she became an alcoholic. My grandfather told me that after she got pregnant, and could not get an abortion, she moved in with her boyfriend, my father. After she left, my grandfather told me that he found dozens of empty vodka bottles hidden in the barn. After that, she could not help herself, she became a hard-core alcoholic, and drug addict. When my mom had me, she brought me to my grandmother's house so she could raise me. Soon after that, my grandmother died, I was just a baby, and I had to go back to my mother's care.

My father had grown up with a single mother. My grandfather, my father's dad, became an aviator during the Second World War. He was British, and my grandmother was Mexican. She was beautiful and had a great figure. My grandfather died during the Second World War. After he died, my grandmother started going out with this pimp, and my grandmother went into prostitution. My father had a terrible childhood watching men going in and out of the house, with very little respect for his mother. My father's sister July went to live with one of my grandfather's sisters, but she died when my aunt July was 15. My aunt came to live with my father, where she learned to become an alcoholic. Later she moved in with her boyfriend. My father never finished high school. He was arrested a couple times for possession of drugs. He got involved with gangs, and selling drugs. That gave him money to spare, but as he got more and more into drugs and alcohol, he and my mother were always drunk and stoned, and the dealer that provided the drugs for him to sell, did not trust him to sell drugs anymore, so that cut off their money.

When my father started living with my mom, after she had me, they had to sell my mom's car so they could survive. After the money was gone, they started to live on welfare and food stamps.

I hated everybody. When I was eleven, I stole a sling shot and began to shoot at every dog and cat in the neighborhood. I was a good shot. I shot birds, and when they hit the ground, I enjoyed watching them die. I tried not to get caught, but I hit the neighbor's cat on the head, and the cat died. They called the police. Someone had seen me with the sling shot weeks before. She told the police that she thought I was a troublemaker, a boy capable of doing this. The police asked her: did you see him kill the cat? She said no. The police came to our house. I had to go to the police station with my half-drunk mother. She told them that I did not have a sling shot, and that I stayed in my room playing video games all day. The officer asked me if I had a sling shot. I told him no. He said that Shelly had seen me with a sling shot several weeks before. I had a sling shot, I told him, but I lost it. I have not seen it in months. He asked me if I had anything to do with the death of the cat. He said the cat was bleeding from the side of the head when they found it. I told him I knew nothing about it.

The officer asked my mom, where is your husband? He is working, she said. It was a big fat lye. He was passed out on the couch at home. The following week, they stopped him while driving drunk. It was his third DUI. The judge gave him six months in jail.

When I was 14, my evilness got more sophisticated. I started going to the jogging trail where people from the neighborhood ran their dogs, and there were kids with their skateboards, and runners were often seen. At first, I would watch the beautiful girls in their short shorts, and tight buts. They looked like they were so happy, listening to their music, as they run down the path. I wanted to let lose my sexual rage, which I began to have when I was fourteen years old. I had nothing but envy and anger, and hatred. I knew I had to do something. I would take my sling shot, I would hide, then hit the girls on the butt, not real hard, and then appear like a Good Samaritan, and would call 911 for them, if they wanted. I only did it a couple times. I was afraid to get caught. The officer that had interrogated me when I was eleven years old, responded to this call as well. I wonder if he recognizes me. He did, and he had child protective services officers visit my house.

When the officers from the child protective services knocked on the door, no one answered. The officer looked through the window on the side, he could see both of my parents on the couch, passed out. He went back to the door, and pounded on the door hard, and said: "This is the police, please open the door. When my father came to the door, he was unstable as he walked to open the door. I was on top of the stairs watching all of this play out. The two officers introduced themselves, and asked: where is Ricky? I came down the stairs, and said: here I am. The officers looked around the room, and in the kitchen. It was all a mess. He opened the refrigerator. There was only beer. The officer asked me: have you eaten today? No, I said, my mom is going to the market later.

They tried talking to my parents, but they could not understand them, they were obviously intoxicated and had slurred speech. The officer then told them that they were taking me into their custody, until there was an investigation and a ruling by the Judge to decide where I would go.

My parents were happy to see me go. They did not have to worry about me anymore. When they received their welfare money, however, they got less money because I did not live with them. That unsettled them.

They placed me in foster care with a nice family, the Brown family. It was incredible how a nice family lived. There was no alcohol in the house. They treated each other with respect and love, and dignity. Everything was in total order, and friendliness. From the beginning they treated me as part of the family. They all wanted me to feel welcome.

I had never felt so good. It seemed I finally had a family. All of this was exactly the opposite of what I really wanted. I wanted to hurt people, I wanted to violently rape a girl and watch her agonize while I threatened her with a knife. These were my fantasies.

They had a beautiful teenage daughter Franny. She had a heavenly body. She was fifteen, just like me. She had a younger brother Jim. For a minute I thought I could leave all this hatred, anger, and violence behind. But soon, evil thoughts were coming into my head. I began stealing from them, mostly money. When they confronted me, I always denied it.

One Saturday afternoon, there was no one home, except for Franny and me. I was walking down the hall; she had her bedroom door open. She said hello, I said hello, and can I come in? Come in she said. She was sitting on the bed writing in her diary. I sat on the chair next to the bed. Suddenly I got this unstoppable feeling, and I jumped on top of her on the bed. She was very quick and got off the bed on the other side in a split second. She kept her cool and helped to defuse the situation.

She said to me that I could not live with them if I ever did that to her ever again. For a minute I thought of jumping her again, but I contained myself. I told her I was sorry, and walked into my room.

Franny documented in her diary what had happened to her that afternoon but decided not to tell her parents about the ordeal. Franny was a kind and gentle soul. She thought she could help me be a better person.

Prior to my arrival into the home, the parents had told their children about the sad history of my life. Franny felt sorry for me.

From the beginning the family tried to develop a friendly relationship with me. Franny was hopeful that with my exposure to this kind, honorable, and loving family, I would change all the sadness of my past, and it would help me develop a brighter honorable future for me. After all, this was the dream of the brown family when they entered this program to help a teenager in trouble have a better chance for a decent life.

I was failing in High school. I was always in the principal's office. They changed me from room to room. Things got so bad; they had to expel me. I didn't care if I passed or failed. It seemed like a great playground to watch these beautiful girls that might become my victims.

When I was sixteen, my parents got me back. They had gone through rehabilitation, and asked for custody of me, I never understood why. The judge gave them custody.

Now I understand why they wanted me back. They would get more money from welfare if they had me back.

After I killed my grandfather some years back, my mom was the only err. It took a long time for my Grandparent's estate to be resolved. She had inherited my Grandparents farm, all the tractors, the cattle, the money in the bank, it was all hers. My mother and father were never married. They did not know how to manage all this money. To begin with the lawyers, they hired figured out that they were drug addicts, and they took advantage of them in every way they could. That is why it took so long for them to finally get the money and property. They also had a realtor that collaborated with the attorneys that my parents hired. They were hired to sell the farm. Either way my parents ended up with millions of dollars.

The Seco saloon and bar were for sale. Katy and Pete were in their seventies and wanted to sell the saloon. They had owned it for more than forty years. They had four children, but none of them wanted to take over the family business. Their kids had seen how hard and dedicated their parents had to be to maintain it. Pete, or Katy had to be there to close the saloon almost every night. It closed at eight on weekdays, and at midnight on the weekends, except Sundays. Over the years they had made a fortune. It was the best and most prestigious restaurant bar in town. It was always full, and it was due to their hard work and dedication.

With the same real estate agent my parents bought the Seco saloon and bought a real nice house. They bought a new Cadillac, and a Harley motorcycle. The Seco saloon had twenty employees. It was a classy place, where the upper middle class came to eat, and had a good time. Every weekend they had live music, and danced in front of the bar. They had great food, and a beautiful bar. On the weekends they had three bar tenders. It was like an icon in town. It gave my parents great immense pride in being the owners.

To make the Seco Saloon function, the owners had to have dedication and discipline. They must organize their business so that every product they will need will be there at the right time. They had to buy vegetables, meat, beverages, liquor, cleaning products that were needed every day. The saloon had a manager that helped with managing the business. He had been working for ten years, and he knew how to run the business, but the owner had to be on top to make sure everything ran smoothly. There were cooks, the waters, the bare tenders, the dish washers, and the cleaning crew. The bathrooms had to be perfectly clean. They had college kids that did the valet parking. The owners had to coordinate and pay them all. It was a big job, with big responsibilities. The owners of the saloon had to pay the different providers, of food, liquor, cleaning supplies, flowers, decorations, musicians, light, water, gas, insurance, wages, and employs benefits, and taxes. My parents had no idea what they had gotten into.

My parents were having a great life spending money, but had no clue how to run a business, or even a household. All day they asked the bartender to make them exotic drinks, and by closing time they were drunk, and sometimes the employees had to take them home.

They were going on expensive vacations. They were going to expensive casinos. They thought the money would never end.

Three months after buying the seco saloon they went out of business and had to sell the place for nearly nothing. They had no idea what they were doing. All they cared about was getting loaded. When the money ran out, they took a loan on the house. Then, they could not pay the loan. They ended up losing the house. My dad had an accident while under the influence of alcohol and totaled the Cadillac. Now they have nothing.

And now, I was living in this rented house, and I fantasize about violently, raping a girl. In my room, all I did was lift weights, then I would run around the block. I had porno magazines and movies. I bought all this with the money I had stolen from my neighbors when we lived in the big house. I was jacking off all the time. It's like I had an overdose of testosterone.

I came home; my parents were doping themselves downstairs. I went in the Kitchen and got a knife. I tried all the knives to see which one I liked and was more comfortable with. I was always looking for some animal to kill. For a minute, I considered killing my parents, but at the last minute, I chickened out.

I finally graduated from High school. The Seco High School got rid of me. They did not know what to do with me, they could not take it anymore, they wanted me out, and so they graduated me.

I was nineteen years old; I joined the Marines. After basic training, they sent me to the Afghanistan war. I moved up the ranks and did not have any trouble confronting the enemy. After a year's tour during the Afghanistan war, I requested a second, then a third tour. I was thirty years old when I was finally discharged from the Marines with honors.

They were looking for a chief of police in Seco, Texas where I grew up. I applied for the job. The only discipline and positive experiences I had had in my life was in the military. I was highly recommended by my commanding officer who lived in Seco. He was a coronel at the nearby marine base. I guess coming home as a hero made many forget my high school years. They gave me the job, and we turned a new page.

Of course, they didn't know what only a couple of my fellow soldiers knew, the savage, unnecessary killings that I had done while in the military. They cheered me on. They called me fearless. Of course, I wanted my life to be in danger to enjoy the fury of the kill.

I started going to a Methodist church in Seco and began to feel as a part of the community. The daughter of the preacher was the most beautiful girl in town, and I married her. She entered my heart, and I never had anything but love and kindness towards her. We had two kids, and something happened to me as a family man. There was no hatred or anger towards my family, there was no limit to the attention I would give my family and my closest friends to maintain an image of an honorable authority. There was always my protection and, love towards them. They did not know about the sexual rage, and anger that was always burning in me, that I had to contain. Of course, I had to always keep an honorable, and dignified image in the community, so I had to do things very carefully. I knew my training while in the Marines was going to help me.

Now my parents are proud of me because I am the Chief of Police. I don't want to have any relationship with them. I am angry with them because of all the sadness I had growing up. I was always covering up for them with the police, and the child protective services when I was growing up. They never cared about me. I was just a stone in their shoes. They never gave me any love, or any attention, or any direction for my life. I just existed in their house on my own. I was a bother to them. I was in the way. They could not wait for me to leave, so that I would be out of their house, and jurisdiction, that way they would not have to worry about me. My mother told me that the pregnancy she had was an accident. She did not want to ever be pregnant. She was only sixteen years old and did not graduate from high school. When she discovered she was pregnant, she was three months alone, and she could not get an abortion. When she turned eighteen, she had her tubes tied, so she could never get pregnant again. She began to use drugs, and alcohol, when she was fourteen years old. My father was ten years older than her. He was the one who introduced her to the use of drugs and alcohol that became her addiction, her passion, and her God. She discovered that she could not live without them. At the age of fifteen, she became an alcoholic. After she began using drugs, and alcohol, there was no turning back.

When they refused to do an abortion, she wanted to go into Mexico nearby to have an abortion, but my grandmother did not permit it. My grandmother was a religious person, but she was a chain smoker. She had emphysema and was weak. She tried to take care of me when I was born, but she died one year later. My grandparents lived in a farm, my grandfather was unable to take care of a baby, so my mother, who was then living with my father had to take over my care. Few years later when I was older, I went to live with my grandfather, until I killed my loving Grandfather. He was the only one that loved me.

Now that I am the chief of police, my parents are enormously proud of me, and of course this gave them a certain status in the community. As the years went by, they both were in and out of jail, mostly for drug and alcohol related issues. I was always very embarrassed to see them, so I never went to see them, not in their house, or in jail.

Because of their erratic, and drug related lifestyle, they could not keep a job, and they were always on welfare and food stamps which they used to buy beer, and drugs. My father was caught during an arm robbery. I was called to the seen, and had to bring him in. I testified in the trial. My father was fifty-nine years old and had the beginning of cirrhosis of the liver. Because of his previous and frequent visits to court, the judge gave him twenty-five years, without the possibility of parole. While waiting for trial he had to be hospitalized twice because of severe alcohol withdrawal syndrome at first, and later because of cirrhosis related problems. After his trial, he was sent to jail. While in jail, he started to turn yellow and had frequent visits to the hospital. He began vomiting blood, and his abdomen became distended. He looked like he was pregnant. I had to go in the jail to take him in and out of the hospital. Two years later he died, and his misery finally ended. There were only a few people at his burial, most of them were his drinking buddies, and others he had met during the multiple times he had been in jail.

My mother, who always looked and acted much younger than her age, was there with her new boyfriend she had met at a bar while my father was in jail. They looked like they were drunk and stoned. They thought they were at a party. My mother's new boyfriend was a Mexican drug dealer and had been in jail before for selling drugs. He was a member of a cartel that dealt with drugs, prostitution, and money laundering. He was well known to the law enforcement community. My parents, when they were young, were very good looking, and were intelligent, but got into the drugs and alcohol culture with their friends early in life, and that changed their lives forever. They lost their ambition. Alcohol was their God, and everything in their lives revolved around that. The only friends they had, were in the same culture, and if they did not fest in alcohol and drugs, they did not belong.

She went to live with her new boyfriend in El Paso. Two years later, they were both killed by rival gangs that shot them both, while in his house.

Years had passed, and I began to look for my first victim, after becoming the chief of police. I had the police car, and as part of my job, I wandered all over town looking, spying, and trying to discover an opportunity. I started thinking of where I could carry out these assaults and started purchasing the items I thought I would need. I always purchased my equipment out of town. The assault had to be where there were no witnesses and leave no evidence. I had to figure out where I would dump the evidence, and make sure that I didn't leave my DNA evidence behind. All of this was always roaming through my mind every minute, of every day. The one thing I knew for sure was that I could not get caught and ruin my family's life in that way. They admired me.

I went into the desert on my motorcycle looking for the perfect spot to commit my crimes.

I had so many advantages; I worked whenever I wanted to. The people often saw me roaming around at night, talking with police, and trying to do my job, but I was really looking for my prey.

My first victim was Ana. Ana was a 26-year-old single mother that lived with her roommate. She was an excellent student while attending Seco Junior College, where she met her husband. He later became an officer in the army during the Afghanistan War. After having twin daughters, she became a stay home Mom looking after her daughters. Her husband was deployed to Afghanistan, where he was killed during a suicide explosion. She started working the night shift at the Seco Café, after her husband's death. Her roommate looked after her two daughters at night while Ana was working the night shift, and her roommate worked during the day, and Ana took care of the girls during the day.

When she worked the nightshift at the Seco Café, she always parked her car in back, in the employees' parking. I began to sleep in the police station on my office couch for a few nights. I had a very understanding wife, and family. At night I would visit the Seco café, come in for a cup of coffee, while Anna worked the night shift. I began to have fantasies, I knew I was going to have her, I just had to figure out when, and where. I made friends with her, and I was always asking questions that would help me in planning when I would strike. Then I began stocking her. I wanted to know which her car was. How she got in, and out of the car, and did she come alone. What did she usually carry with her, and what is her usual time to get into her car after the night shift, and if there were other people around. I waited and looked for the perfect night when she was leaving after all of the employees had left. It was on Tuesday that she locked up, I figured that out by stocking her. I had to see if there were security cameras and were. I couldn't wait. My fantasies were pushing me.

It was my time to strike. I was ready. I had my gloves, my mask, and disposable clothing on. I was wearing a green surgical disposable gown. I had no underwear, and of course, I had the gun that I had stolen when I was a teenager from one of my neighbor's houses. I had my military knife. I had my powerful LED lights. I was ready.

I hid behind her car; I had already disconnected the lights inside her car. I had cut the wires of the surveillance cameras first. I hid along the wall, where the cameras could not see me, and cut the wire.

She arrived at her car and unlocked the car. I came in from the passenger side. I immediately put my hand over her mouth and face and took complete control of her. I turned her cell phone off. I threatened her to death with my gun, if she made another sound. I ordered her to drive out of the parking lot, then turned right. She began to drive. I sat on the floor of the passenger side; I didn't want anyone to see that there was someone else in the car. I pointed the gun at her head.

Seco Texas got its name because it is in the middle of the desert. There are miles and miles of desert. Many places where I could hide and not be seen. I was very good with disguises; I had my especial equipment that I would use when I was going to strike. I knew the rules, and I had been preparing for this moment for years. I will be able to finely experience this sexual rage that is in me, that I have been dreaming of, and is anxious to erupt.

I loved motorcycles, I had two. I had rigged one of them, the smallest one. The one that made the least noise, and no one liked it. I rigged a broom over the front, and rear tires fenders to erase the tire marks left by the motorcycle, and that way, not leave any evidence.

I made my boots myself, so there were no traceable shoe prints. I had a basement in my house that I had expanded, under the house. It took me years to do it, but I did it just the way I wanted. I always kept it locked. I had a hiding room, behind the counter in the second room of the basement, it was impossible to find, and difficult to get into. It was a room imbedded in cement. I had running water, and electricity. It had TV cable, and a TV. It had access to the cameras that showed me who entered the house, and it showed me if they were trying to enter my basement. There were two computers, and electronic equipment. There was counter space, drawers, and documents. Since we lived on a hill, I was able to have a small bathroom with a sink that I connected to the sewer that drained by gravity.

Imbedded on the wall of my hidden room, I had a hidden security safe, with a specific, and complicated electronic code.

I let my friends and family into the first room of my basement. It was the "boy's room". In the front room, I had a big screen TV, a refrigerator, a microwave, and a music system. In the second room behind, it was private. I had all kinds of tools on the wall, and on the counters. It was a large room. I had grinders, large drills screw drivers of every kind. Machines to work with tile, wood, and a welder to work with metal. I had learned all these skills, while in the Marines in Afghanistan. There, I couldn't just call the plumber or the electrician, so I had to learn to do all these things myself. Because of the foundation of the house, I could keep that part of the basement separated, and keep it locked when I wanted. It was in this back area that I had the entrance to my secret room. No one had ever seen it. Either way, I kept all my basement locked, and no one ever went in, unless I was present.

While looking in the desert, I found the remains of someone's attempts to build a small room. It had a fire pit. It was 5 Kilometers from highway 5E, that entered from the northeast, and about 7 miles to the fork of the 2W highway, and desert center road, which come in from the west. I needed a hiding spot, where I could hide my tool kit, where I could hide things like my broom for the motorcycle, knifes, my gun, latex gloves, and other paraphernalia needed for my assault. That way I could always pick up the right tool for the job and not keep them in the house. I found the perfect spot, between the two main roads to hide my box in the desert. I dug a hole in the ground, then covered it with some plywood and poured sand on top of it. Inside along with my equipment, I had an electronic chip, that way I could find it with my GPS when I wanted to.

I had shaved my head, and all my body, including using mirrors to shave between my balls, and all pubic hair, that way I would not leave a hair behind. I was sure I could commit the perfect crime.

One more thing that has given me an advantage. After the

birth of my second child, I had a vasectomy done, and last year, after having an enlarged prostate, they had to remove it with this new technology, green laser. This made me have retrograde ejaculation. Nothing comes out from my penis when I ejaculate.

I had my motorcycle waiting. I was dreaming about this night. How should I make her suffer? Should I give her some hope, then see the severe fear and anguish in her face.

After a couple of minutes of driving, I could tell we had left the pavement. I made her make a U turn; I sat up we went back to HWY 2W. She drove for a couple of miles. There was no one around. I ordered her to get off the road, and we drove over fairly hard packed sand in the desert. I ordered her to stop. I have a great since of direction. I never get lost. I took the keys from the car and placed them on the floor. I came around the driver's side and took my knife out. I ordered her to take all of her clothing off. I had come earlier to hide my motorcycle and place a tarp and the light where it would all take place.

I hit her on the head and dragged her on top of the tarp. I then turned the lights on. She begged for her life. Please, she said, "I have two little girls. Then she tried to scratch me. Finely, I took my knife, and slit half of her throat, so that I could hear her agonizing as she fought for her life. I got this stiff erection; I had never had anything like that before. I heard her making these gurgling noises, as she was taking her last final breaths, as she was choking on her blood. I went into her dry vagina, and pushed my dick inside of her, as I watched her die. I then had a horrendous orgasm and began to shake for a long time afterward. I could not move; I had to wait for all this rage to come out of me.

After it was all over, I took my knife and cut off her left nipple and placed it in a small plastic bag I had brought. I took all of her clothing, and my plastic gown, mask, and shoe cover, and all the evidence, and placed it in the middle of the tarp. I rolled her body off the tarp. I then rolled the tarp up and placed it all in a large plastic bag. I Left the car just as it was. I destroyed any shoe marks. Made sure there was no blood on me. I left the body in the same position it had landed after I rolled her off the tarp. I then jumped from bush to bush trying not to live shoe marks. Finely I got to my motorcycle, I went to the remote fire pit, I poured alcohol over the bag with the tarp, and burned all the evidence including her phone. After it all had burned, I put sand over the fire pit, and drove to my hiding place, where I kept my equipment, I cleaned my knife, and gun, and everything I had come in contact, with alcohol on the very remote possibility that someone would find my equipment box in this endless desert. I put on my close and drove back to the police station on my motorcycle. It was only 12 P.M. In Seco, everybody is in bed by 8 P.M.

Later, I went home, and into my secret room. I opened my safety box. I took a pin and put it through the center of the nipple. I wrote her name and the date on a small piece of paper and put the paper through the pin in the nipple, and placed the nipple in a jar, in my safety box.

The next day her roommate called Ana's parents to ask if Ana had spent the night with them. Her mother said no. It was really unusual for Ana not to come home. Her roommate said that she had to go to work, and she needed to leave the girls with them. The roommate then drove to the Saco Cafe to see if she had normally worked the night before, and if anyone had seen her leave. They called Marsha, who worked the night shift with Ana. They asked her if she had seen Ana leave that night. Marsha said everything was normal. Marsha said she had left the café before Ana. Ana was going to lock up.

The owner of the Saco café tried to see what had happened and discovered that all of his security cameras had been cut. He looked at the recordings but could not figure out who cut the wires. Ana's parents, and Marsha went to the police department to file a missing person report. I told them that they had to wait 48 Hrs. to file the missing person report. I said I would talk with the police officers, to be on the look out to see if anyone had seen her car or know of her whereabouts.

Forty-eight hours passed, and of course there was no Ana. The missing person's report was filed, and as usual, the report was sent to the county sheriff. There was no sign of Ana. The investigation was in the hands of the Saco police chief, the county sheriff, and detectives. The cable news reported this unusual event in Seco Texas. There was a missing woman.

There had never been a homicide in the history of the city. The County sheriff, and another crime specialist came to Seco to investigate. They could not find her phone. It was off. They went to the phone company, to see what phone calls she had made, and where she had called, but none of the leads helped them with the case.

Days went by, then months, and no one seem to know the whereabouts of Ana. Her parents came to the police station almost every day to see if we knew anything new about Ana. Of course, the answer was always the same. There was nothing new in Ana's investigation. Her parents were devastated, but no one had seen her, and no one had any idea where she had gone. The police had not found even a shred of evidence of her whereabouts.

I guess no one talked about Ana's disappearance anymore, except for her parents, who came to ask about her frequently. Her case seemed to be forgotten. As months went by, Anna's folder was placed in the unresolved case files.

I now started thinking and looking for my next victim. It was Betty. She was one of the cheer leaders at Seco High School. She was truly beautiful. I saw her one evening smoking marijuana inside her car, on her way to the Friday night High School football game. I knew there and then that she would be my next victim.

Marijuana has always been illegal in Texas. Every Friday night she bought marijuana from an out-of-town drug dealer. I had been stocking her for a while. I knew that every Friday, before going to the game, she purchased Marijuana from this dealer, then she made a joint, and smoked it in her car before the game. After the game she got together with her friends to smoke weed. She had been doing this for some time, and I knew it.

It was Friday night. I left my police car at the station. I decided, this was the night. I was ready. I had left my motorcycle near where I intended to do the crime, which was a totally different place than before. The drug dealer that sold her the marijuana always asked her to meet him outside of town, so that he would not be seen selling the drug in town.

I had my gloves on, and was carrying a bag, with the rest of my equipment. She was smoking marijuana in her car just outside of town when I approached her. She was loaded, and playful. I knocked on the passenger window, and she unlocked the door. I came in and told her that I was going to take her in, however, I pulled my gun out and told her to drive out of town. I turned her cell phone off. Again, I sat on the floor on the passenger side, as before, I pointed the gun at her head. She thought it was a big joke and continued to be playful.

I had everything set up. This time I had more experience. We turned into a dirt road off the 5W Hwy. We drove into the desert for about 5 miles. I sat up to have a good look around. We then went off the hard-packed dirt road into the desert, for about a half an hour. It took me a little while to find my tarp. When we got there, I took the car keys and placed them on the floor. I took off all of my clothes, and put them in a plastic bag, then put on my gown. I tried not to leave any DNA from my mouth, so I put on my mask. I had hand cuffed her to the open door. I was ready.

I took my keys and unlocked the hand cuffs that I had used to secure her to the door. I ordered her to take her close off. She said: I'll give you a piece of ass, if you don't take me to jail, and you don't tell my parents about the marijuana. I laughed. She had no clue what was happening to her.

I took my knife out, and she began to scream. She finally realized that I was going to kill her. I took her tongue, pulled it out, and cut it off. She began to bleed profusely, and she was choking and drowning in her own blood. I could hear those gurgling sounds that turned me on. I took my knife and cut her face in half. She went into severe panic. I opened her chest, cut through the bone and could see her heart pumping. This was Disneyland for me. Every move I made gave me great pleasure. I started getting a hard erection. I knew it was time for the kill. I took my knife and stabbed her heart. As she was dying, I went inside her vagina and began to have an incredible orgasm that lasted for a long time, as before, I started shaking violently. When I stopped shaking, I cut off Betty's Left Nipple and placed it in a small plastic bag I brought with me.   I left the car as it was. I pushed her off the tarp, then took my robe off, and my mask, and my gloves, and all of her clothing and placed it on the tarp. I rolled up the tarp and placed it all into a large plastic bag. I looked around to make sure I was not leaving any evidence behind. I put on my clothes, then I jumped around from bush to bush, until I found my motorcycle. I took it all to the incinerator and burned it all as I did before. I stayed until it was all burned, including her phone.

Then I went to my hidden box, about eight miles away. I took some gasoline from my motorcycle. Cleaned everything carefully, making sure I left no prints, in case they found my hidden box. Then I went back to the football game and sat at the game for the fourth quarter. When I got home, I took Betty's left nipple, put a pin through it, and wrote in a small piece of paper Betty's name, and the date. I then placed it in the jar with the other nipple.

It was very rare for Betty no to be present at the game; something must have happened to her. Her best friend had called her several times, but her phone was off.

They started to look everywhere. Her car was not in the parking lot. Her friend went to her house, but her parents said they thought she was at the game.

Desperation took over, after they could not find her. No one had seen her. They went to the police, but I told them that they had to wait 48 Hrs. before they could file a missing person report, however, all the police department was immediately mobilized looking for her and her car.

The report was filed. The county Sheriff and his team began the investigation. They started thinking that there might be a connection between the cases of Ana, eleven months before, and Bettie's case.

After Betty's disappearance, they put more investigators into the case. Her father was an attorney, so they were more diligent. The next morning, they started to do flying zones over the desert in order to find her.

They could not find her, but they were able to find Ana's car, and found Ana's body, half eaten by vaulters, and other animals. It was deteriorated from the sun and the elements. It was clear, however, that the killer had cut off Anna's left nipple, and had slid her throat. The forensic Pathologist said that there was no doubt that this had been done with a knife. They brought some of the best forensic detectives, and pathologists, as well as the FBI to investigate the case. There were no tire tracks. The wind with time had blown the tire tracks away. Of course, I, as the chief of police in Seco, had jurisdiction over the case. Ana's parents had finely gotten closure, and they were able to bury what was left of Ana's body. There were no forensic clues. After making final notes and pictures, months later, I placed her file back in the unsolved homicide cases.

The forensic pathologist was able to discover that Ana had a violent death. There was no evidence of rape. They were unable to find any evidence that the nipple was removed by an animal or insects, or birds. It had been done by a sharp object that had also slid her throat. It had the same serrated pattern.

The car was taken to the forensic laboratory to be processed by the investigators, but they could not find any clues.

They were unable to find Betty's body. The press was all over this case. In a town like Seco Texas, there had been another missing person, and a possible second homicide.

Two days later, a helicopter spotted Betty's car. Immediately, I, along with several other agents, drove to the seen to inspect the site. The tire marks were still visible, and we were able to trace them to the hard pack desert road, where they could not be identified any longer. A perimeter was formed. The forensic experts went over her body and car to see if they could get some forensic clues. No fingerprints were found, other than her family and friends. Her car was taken to the forensic lab for further inspection. They found a small plastic bag with marijuana. They took the bag for forensic analysis.

Betty's autopsy, aside from revealing a missing left nipple there were no other useful clues. The toxicology studies showed that she had marijuana in her blood, as well as a small amount of alcohol. There was evidence of the brutal attack to her face that was cut in half. Her chest was open. Her heart had been brutally stabbed. They also discovered that her tongue had been cut at the base. The tongue was later found nearby. Though there were lots of trauma to her legs, and abdomen, there was no semen. This made the possibility of rape more remote, however, there was some evidence that there might have been forceful penetration into her vagina. There had been obvious and severe brutal trauma.

Their only clue was the small bag with Marijuana. Fingerprints were found in the bag, some were hers, but others were foreign. After the detectives interviewed all of her friends, one by one, there were no helpful hints, until the detectives decided to tell her friends that they had found a small bag with marijuana in the car. Finely, her best friend confided in the police and told them that every Friday she bought marijuana from an out-of-town dealer.

The fingerprints from the bag were lifted and put into the FBI data base and were immediately able to discover who they belong to. This drug dealer had been previously in jail for selling drugs.

They were able to find the drug dealer and they took him to the Seco police department for an interview. I conducted the first interview, it was recorded. The forensic pathologist was able to figure out the time of death for Betty, and it coincided well with the time Fernando, the drug dealer, had testified that he sold Betty the marijuana. They had Fernando, the drug dealer, take off all his clothing to see if he had any scratches, or bruises. He had none. They looked in his apartment, and car to see if there was any blood or sand in his shoes, or blood in his clothing. They took his car in for a forensic inspection. They found nothing.

Fernando told the police that he had sold Betty the marijuana, but she was happy, and well. He said that she asked him if he wanted to smoke a Joint with her, but he told her he had to run. I did not want to be seen in town, and he said he did not have anything to do with her murder. They asked him to take a polygraph test, which he did, and passed with flying colors. He was then discarded as a suspect.

They had no other suspects; they brought in other experts and could not find the killer.

Weeks went by, then months, and I finally placed her folder in the unresolved missing person's case file. No one asked about Betty anymore.

The news reporters started calling me the serial nipple killer, of course, they did not have the slightest idea that it was really me. I liked the attention and made me more determined to have my next victim.

I started looking for my next victim. My next victim was Carola. Carola was the daughter of an undocumented Mexican family that had a house just outside of town. She was fourteen years old, but like many other Mexican girls, she was well developed and had this beautiful virgin tits. When I saw her walking home, I knew she would be my next victim.

I had usually looked for a girl that had a car, so that I could use it to transport us to the scene of the crime. Carola did not have a car. This complicated things. Usually, it took me months of planning to make sure all would go well. With Carola, I got a hard on just watching her walk.

I began to stock her. I would go by on my police car and would talk to her when she walked home. It was about a mile walk. I began to make friends with her and would act like it was a coincidence that we would run into each other. I was always asking her questions to be better informed. She admired and trusted me as an authority. She walked home along a very deserted and dark pedestrian path, but in Seco there was never any danger. I discovered that every Wednesday, she walked to her church for quire practice that met at seven, then she walked home.

I got ready for Wednesday. I put everything in motion. I decided I would ask her if I could take her home when she was walking home after quire practice.

I was on my motorcycle, and after she was in the dark part of her walk, I appeared and asked her if I could give her a ride home. She agreed, and she hopped on the back.

I started driving, and when she discovered I was not going to her house, she began to shake the motorcycle, pounding on my back, and asking me to stop. I stopped and took my knife out and rubbed it against the side off her face. I told her not to make any trouble, or I would cut off her throat. I tied her to the motorcycle.

I drove to where I had already placed my tarp. I tied her to the motorcycle with my hand cuffs, while I took off my clothing, and put on my gown and mask. I already had my gloves on. I then took off the hand cuffs. I asked her to take off all her clothing. She started to run. I chased her down with the motorcycle and hit her hard on the back of the head with my gun. She fell, and I drugged her back. Again, I asked her to take off her clothing, but she refused. I took my knife and cut off her leg completely, so she could not run. She was already on the tarp. I took all of her clothing off. She was losing a lot of blood from her leg. I started sucking her virgin tits. She passed out. I was very disappointed. I opened her abdomen. She was already dead.

I was very angry with myself. I did everything wrong. I did not get off. I cut off her left nipple, I rolled her off the tarp, took all of the evidence, and burned it. It had been very bloody. I made sure that all the blood had not contaminated me. After placing my equipment in my box, I cleaned my box to make sure I left no prints. I drove my motorcycle home. My wife was not home; she had gone to the market. I washed my motorcycle. I went into my secret room and placed a pin through her nipple and put her name, and the date, and placed it inside the jar.

Suddenly I heard someone pounding at the door screaming. It was Carola's mother. She was crying and screaming. Her daughter had not come home. She said Carola had gone to church, but she had not returned. Carola was not at the church, and she could not find her.

I tried to calm her down and told her that Carola had probably gone with one of her friends and would probably appear soon. I asked her if there were any problems with her. She told me no, her daughter was a very good girl, and if she was going to go anywhere, she would have told her. I could not calm her down. She told me her husband had gone to work and would not be back until Saturday.

The door opened, and in came my wife and my two kids. I asked my wife if she could take Carola's Mom to the church to see if the priest could console her. I told my wife that she was concerned about the disappearance of her daughter.

The convulsion reiterated through the town, and everyone came out to see what was happening. Carola's mother screamed at the top of her lungs with horror and desperation. The neighbors began to organize themselves to see if they could find Carola. All night they looked through the town, and desert to see if they could find her, but no one could. I organized the police to look for her in another area, but unfortunately, she was nowhere to be found.

Again, a missing girl in Seco. The county Sheriff, and other crime detectives, as well as the FBI began the investigation. The next morning, air surveillance found her body. Though I thought I had hidden all the blood evidence, they found a pool of blood that had drained from her leg. Her leg was a few feet from the body, and it was evident that vaulters had been devouring part of her leg and body. This made it more difficult to find forensic evidence, however, there was clear evidence that her left nipple had been cut off with a knife.

Her abdomen had been opened, and it looked like it was done with the same knife; this had not been done by animals.

The detectives cordoned off the crime scene. They noticed the marks on the sand, where she had been obviously dragged. They could see on the desert ground where the crime had been committed. They could tell I was using a tarp to hide the evidence. They also noticed the motorcycle tire marks erased by the broom. It was obvious that someone was trying to erase the tire tracks. The marks went around the different dessert shrubs, and they could not trace them very far.

The forensic pathologist that did the autopsy discovered that she had been hit hard on the back of the head, causing a skull fracture. Her abdomen had been opened with a knife. They could tell that the same knife serrated pattern, had cut off her leg, and her left nipple. They looked at pictures of the other two cases, and with magnification they could tell that the knife serrations were similar to the other two cases. With the left nipple gone, it was obvious it had been done by the nipple killer. Experts were brought in to review the pictures of the other victims, there was no doubt that the same knife had cut off the nipples of the previous victims. It had the same serrated patterns.

The newspapers on the front page said: the nipple killer strikes again. I was sitting on my desk reading the newspaper with much interest. Now the whole town is on the lookout for the nipple killer.

I was giving courses on what to look for, and how to defend yourself from the serial nipple killer.

I was getting a lot of attention from the press. They came from everywhere to interview me. I really liked the attention, and I was very proud to offer my opinion on the different scenarios that might explain what was taking place. I told them that it had to be a very sick person to do this. I would say, it had to be a sicko from out of town that was hurting our defenseless women. I would say: I am sure we will catch him soon.

Seco was one of the largest towns near the Texas Mexican border. We were close to a Marine base, and many of the citizens worked at the base. We had a good hospital in town, a large police force, a fire department, a community college, a great high school with a winning football season. We had lawyers, Doctors, Dentist, engineers, plumbers, carpenters, gardeners, and many other professionals and workers. We had several elegant malls. We had a great community. People from other nearby small towns came to our shopping malls, our hospital, and to our community college, Seco Junior college. It was a middle-class community.

About thirty miles southwest there was a small town called Arroyo Texas. It was called that, because they had a large natural spring that made its way through the middle of town, and made everything green in the desert. There were palm trees, flowers, and a small lagoon nearby. It was where the rich from El Paso Texas had their vacation homes. Many wealthy retired people lived in town. It had several markets, pharmacies, malls and many restaurants. There was also a community of Mexican families that were living on the other side of this old town that dated back centuries. These individuals did the gardening, the cleaning, and whatever manual labor was needed in the community. There was an old small school attended mainly by the Hispanic community. They lived in a separate poor part of Arroyo. I decided to pick my next victim from Arroyo. When I had some free time, I would go to Arroyo, on my motorcycle looking for possibilities. With my motorcycle helmet, no one could tell who I was.

Most of the Mexican kids walked to school. They had to walk about a mile and a half to get to school. I wanted to show the press that this sicko that was committing these murders was from out of town. I started looking around for my next victim. My next victim was Dorita. She was only twelve years old. She appeared slower than the other kids, but she was well developed.

She always walked alone. There was a part of her daily walk that was deserted. There was little traffic, and it was unusual to see pedestrians around, other than the kids walking to school.

I started to develop my plan. I decided to use my personal car. I forced her into the car. As usual I had everything ready. I drove a couple of miles where my motorcycle was waiting. There was no one around. She fought me, but I tied her to the motorcycle so that she would not run. Driving through the desert on my motorcycle I started to think how I would enjoy seeing her suffer. I brought her to the tarp I had set up. I had her tied to the motorcycle with my hand cuffs. I took my clothing off, then I ordered her to take her clothing off. I had put on my mask and gloves before I picked her up. She refused to take off her clothing. I started to take out my knife, and as I turned to get it, she took off my mask. I grabbed my knife and stabbed both of her eyes. She started screaming, and I stabbed her in the throat. She began to make the gurgling sounds that turned me on. I got a hard erection. I took her panties off and went inside of her. It was hard to penetrate; she was just a girl. She started bleeding from her vagina. I started having an orgasm that lasted a long time, then I began to shake severely. I was having trouble breathing. I thought I would never stop. Suddenly I became frightened that I might have left DNA on her hand after she took off my mask. I also thought that some of the cells from my penis might have mixed with the blood from her vagina. I cut all of her finger tips off. Though she was just a girl, her breasts were well developed. I took her left nipple and cut it off. I placed it in a small plastic bag. Then I got some gasoline from my motorcycle and put it inside her vagina. I rolled her off the tarp and lit her on fire. As usual, I took all of the evidence, including her fingertips and burned it all in the fire pit. I had the car and the motorcycle that I had to bring home. This complicated things.

My wife had started to think there was something wrong.

I had been using the motorcycle during working hours. I had taken the family car, when she wanted to pick up the kids from school. Calls had come in from the police station looking for me. I had to suddenly make excuses for my absence, and why I was using the family car, and where was my motorcycle.

I told her that I had been having some problems with the motorcycle, and I had to pick up the mechanic, to take the motorcycle to the shop.

I was a master of disguise. When I set things up, I took the motorcycle to the hiding place, and came back to seco, on the bus. I was bald, and had put on a wig and a mustache, and had made some wrinkle marks on my forehead so that no one would recognize me. I had done this two days before.

It appeared that my wife was not buying my story. She had never questioned me before, so she just let things go. When I hid my motorcycle, I always unplugged the spark plug, in case someone wanted to take it.

Later, when my wife was asleep, I went into my safe and entered the nipple into the jar.

The next day, I went by the mechanic and told him I had been having problems with my motorcycle, so we took his trailer, and we picked up my motorcycle.

That afternoon, while my wife was having her massage session, I vacuumed the car to make sure that there were no hair, or other evidence in the car. I wiped off any possibility of her fingerprints being present.

I became afraid, and decided I had to be more careful, but I could not control my appetite. I was not happy with Carola's kill and was desperate for a new victim. However, things went better for me with Dorita, I had a fantastic orgasm. I thought I was going to die.

I decided to cool off for a while, because both my wife and the police department became somewhat suspicious about my whereabouts. I had to control myself.

Within hours Dorita's family noticed that Dorita was missing. She was a little slow mentally, and all her family, and the Mexican community started looking for her. They had a small police department in Arroyo, so they came to us to help them find the girl. She was nowhere to be found.

The police department from Arroyo contacted me immediately. The community was up in arms, desperate to find her. We contacted the county sheriff's office, and the FBI got involved immediately. They did not wait 48 Hrs. as usual.

This time I had placed the body under some bushes so that it would not be so easy to find from the air.

My wife had become more suspicious, and she began to pay attention to my activities. I became aware of her suspicious behavior. She would often ask me where I had been, or where I was going. I had to cool it down. I decided to confront her, and to let her know that I did not like her questioning. I told her that if she had something to say to say it, otherwise to let me do my job, which required investigation to find this killer. Time went by, and she began to relax with her suspicious attitude.

Saturday afternoons, a group of us would often take off on our motorcycles to ride in the desert. One Saturday, I could not go with the group because one of my sons was having a fever, and abdominal pains, I had to take him to the emergency room. He had appendicitis.

The motorcycle riders found Dorita's body, all dried up from the sun. They called me to inform me that they had found her body. I told them not to touch anything, and kept from getting close to the site, until we arrived with the forensic team. I called the county sheriff, the FBI, and the forensic team. They soon arrived at the scene. After exploring the site, they took her half-burned body to the morgue for the forensic autopsy. They discovered that both of her eyes were pocked with a sharp object, and she had been stabbed in the throat. Her left nipple was missing, and again it appeared to have been removed with the same knife. There were very few other clues, since the body had been exposed to the hot sun, and was badly burned, and there was other possible animal intervention. After DNA analysis, they were able to confirm that it was definitely Dorita's body.

Again, the press was all over the case. The nipple killer strikes again. I told them, I was right, this monster is not from our town, he is getting more and more aggressive, but we will find him.

The community was very frightened. They were not permitting the women to be alone. At the church they were having prayer meetings, asking for Gods help. I attended most of the prayer meetings. In public, I would ask the police department, and the community to be vigilant, and to report any suspicious behavior. People were reporting "suspicions individuals", mainly in the Hispanic community. I spent much time interviewing suspects, but all of them either had alibies, or were willing to take the polygraph test, and one by one all of them were eliminated.

The community was agitated, and the suspicion, and the mistrust were destroying the community. Of course, I had the police working overtime, trying to investigate all the calls that were coming in. No one was in peace. Every Sunday the preacher asked the congregation to be cautious, but to not let suspicion turn into hatred and persecution. The restaurants were closing early. The bars were closing at sunset. There was police presence in the emergency room at the hospital. They were suspicious of newcomers, and people that were looking for medical care at the hospital that were from out of town. The police were stopping traffic looking for clues. There was no peace or tranquility in this normally peaceful community.

I decided to lay low for a while. Several months passed, and little by little, the town began to find normalcy.

It had been a year, and I was desperate to find my next victim. It had to be further away. This made it more difficult to operate away from my base. Every day I was looking for my next pray and wondering how I could find my next assault.

There was a police convention in El Paso to see what steps could be taken to catch the nipple killer. This might give me an opportunity, I thought. This meant it had to be a spontaneous event, and not like the other victims where I prepared for weeks to make sure that everything would go well. I was desperate. It had been too long. I wanted blood, and somehow, I was going to get it.

This police convention offered some possibilities. Their focus was on catching the nipple killer, and what we could do as policemen to catch this evil person. The convention was only two days. There would be only one night that I would be away from Seco. I had to act that night. I had to do my best to prepare.

When I arrived, I parked my car in the Hotel parking, and checked in. I was wearing my disguise and used false documents. Then I rented a car using the same disguise, and the same false documents. I stayed in a shady hotel that had a side door near my room. I was at the conference all day, that first day.

At ten P.M. that night, I went into a bar, I could not find any possibilities there, so I kept going from bar to bar, until I found what I thought was the perfect victim. I had put on my disguise, so I would not be identified by witnesses or cameras. It was a cold night, and it was after midnight when I walked into the bar. I saw a half-drunk girl at the bar, obviously looking for company. I had leather gloves on, and a wool hat over my head. We started talking, she wanted action. After buying her a couple drinks, I asked her if she wanted to come to my apartment. By now, she was really drunk, and we went out of the bar. She had slurred speech and had to hang on to me to get into the car. She fell asleep in the car.   I drove into the desert. There was a full moon, and I had fairly good visibility. I had brought some of my tools. I knew this night was my only opportunity. I changed my gloves, and put my mask on. When I stopped the car, she woke up and walked out of the car. I came from behind, and I choked her fairly hard. She fell to the ground. I did not want to kill her jet. I had plans for her. I had to be careful not to have a lot of blood on me, though I still wanted to see blood. I wanted to see fear in her eyes. I took off my close and place them in the car. I had bought a new long knife that I could discard and stabbed her on the side of the neck. She was lying on the ground face down. I stabbed her with such a force with both hands grabbing the knife that went clear through and came out through her mouth, on the other side. I had perforated the trachea. It had been so long since my last victim, I was using all of my force. I knew there had to be blood. She started bleeding and spurting blood. She was choking in her own blood. I heard the gurgling sounds that turned me on. I got a stiff erection, I turned her over, and I took off her panties, and went inside her. It had been a good kill. I had an incredible orgasm. It had been a long time. As usual I began to shake violently. I could not stop. I had blood all over me. Unfortunately, I did not have my tarp. I had been wearing my plastic protective gown. It was difficult to clean up with all this blood. I could not let any of the blood get into the car. I had a large plastic bag with a roll of paper towels, and a second pair of latex gloves. I began to clean up.   I turned the headlights on to clean up. I tried hard not to have any blood on me. I dragged her in front of the car, where I could see her better. I cut off her left nipple.

I put all the evidence into the large plastic bag. I put her panties and clothing into the bag. I carefully put on the second pair of latex gloves, then I put on my clothing, and my disguise.

I went back to the hotel through the back street, and found the dumpster behind a wall, in the back parking lot. First, I looked very carefully to see if they had any cameras over the dumpster area. Than, I took the trash out from the dumpster, and I took the plastic bag and emptied it into the dumpster, including the knife. I separated everything so it would burn rapidly and more importantly, I had seen that it all had burned. I took a small bottle of Alcohol I had brought, and sprinkled some over the items in the bag, and lit them on fire. It took seconds to burn. I was lucky, the dumpster was well hidden. After it burned, I put all the trash back in the dumpster, so it would hide the ashes.

It was five o'clock in the morning. I looked around, and there were no cameras in this posterior part of the hotel parking lot. I drove the car around and entered the hotel from the front. I had my disguise on, I knew they had cameras. I went ininto my room, took a shower and put a fresh shirt and pants on. I put a small plastic bag with the nipple in my shirt pocket. I wiped the hotel room down with alcohol, I did not want to leave any fingerprints. I later took the car I had rented through the car wash; I wiped it clean and took the car back. I walked back to the nearby hotel with my disguise, and I checked out. I had these fine thin leather gloves on. It was a bit cold, but that was not the reason I was wearing them. I left the hotel in my car that I had parked in the hotel parking lot when I first arrived.

I was late to the meeting. They said I should be the most interested police chief there, since the victims were from my area. I told them I had been vomiting all morning but decided to come anyway since I knew this was very important. At the end of the meeting, I drove back in my car to Seco. I was really drained. I did not sleep a wink. My wife noticed I was not acting right. I told her I had been sick all morning. I had a small plastic bag with the nipple in my shirt pocket. When she fell asleep, I took the small bag from my shirt pocket. After writing her name, and date, I placed it in the jar with the other nipples, then went back to my room and fell asleep.

The next morning, my wife had taken my shirt to be washed, unfortunately unbeknown to me, the small plastic bag with the nipple had a tiny hole in it, and had spilled a tiny drop of blood into my shirt pocket. My wife noticed it when she was going to wash the shirt in the morning. She did not wash the shirt and hit it in a box in the garage.

The next day they found the body of the woman I had killed, near El Paso. She had been stabbed in the neck, and her left nipple was gone. This time there were tire tracks. They took molds of the tire tracks and identified the tires as the tires similar to the "factory tires" placed on the new ford mustangs. They began the investigation and found out that the victim had been at the neighborhood bar where she often went with her friends. After inquiring, the police discovered that she had been in the bar, and had left with a man with a mustache, and a wool hat. The investigators were able to see the images that had been captured by the security cameras inside the bar, and in the parking lot that night. The investigators released the story, and the pictures to the news media asking if anyone could identify this man. The hotel clerk recognized the picture right away, and reported it to the police. The hotel had cameras and were able to identify the man. The rent a car man while watching TV, also identified me, and called the police. He reported that I had rented a black mustang from him. They took the car for forensic analysis and found that it had identical tire tracks. No doubt this was the car related to the crime. There were no fingerprints of any kind. It had been whipped clean, however, in the crease of the passenger seat, they found an earring. She was missing an earring, and it match the one found in the car.

At the hotel, the investigators went through the room, but were unable to pick up any prints, or anything useful. I was very careful; however, although there had not any cameras in the back parking lot, the hotel had cameras in the guest parking lot, and they had discovered that I had used a second car. This gave them a big lead. There were no traces of blood in the room, or in the car, and there were no fingerprints. With a clear video of a second car, they knew I had used a second car, and they knew exactly what kind of a second car I had used.

Of course, being the chief of police in Seco, I had the privilege of all the information they were finding. In the hotel parking lot video, they could not see the license plate of my car.

The whole situation was being closely followed by the press. They were interviewing the bar tender, the rent a car man, and the hotel clerk. It was big news, and it was all over the country, especially in town. The press was interrupting normal programing on the TV, as they were getting more and more information. Everybody was on the edge of their seats watching it all unfold. The police had reported that this was the work of the nipple killer. Autopsy showed that her left nipple was gone. I tried to be as careful as I could, hoping they would not find me. This time I had been careless, and had left a lot of evidence, much of which they were not revealing to the public, but of course, as the chief of police, I had all of the information that was being developed.

As everybody in town, including my wife, were glued to the TV, she recognized our car right away. She called the El Paso sheriff's office and asked them not to reveal the source. She told them that she knew who had committed the murder and had the evidence to prove it. She asked them to send an unmarked unit to our house right away, so that she could reveal the evidence. She said that they had to be very careful, because she feared for her life. She asked that the information not be shared with her husband, or the press.

They needed to send someone to our house right away, before something happened to her, she told them.

It was lunch time, and I was coming home for lunch. I knew my wife was going to recognize the car. On TV you could see pictures of our car. It showed a sticker from our Seco high school, the "desert rats", on the back bumper.

I was afraid to come home for lunch, and as I approached the house carefully, I noticed a car in front of the house. I went around the block, parked, and sneaked into the back of the house through the back yard, where I kept the motorcycles. In one of the pockets of the big bike, I had my gun and knife. I slowly sneaked the motorcycle out the back gate and pushed it down the block. I put on my helmet, started my bike, and went out into the desert. Of course, all the pictures of the nipple killer were with a wool hat, and a mustache, it did not fit my discretion. I went to the gas station in Arroyo and filled up my tank.

The El Paso sheriff had arrived in Seco. My wife showed them our car. She took the shirt from the garage and gave it to him. They came to the police department to arrest me, but I was long gone.

They took the car, and the shirt for forensic analysis. The DNA from the drop of blood on the shirt matched the DNA of Elisa, the victim.

Now they had proof beyond a shadow of a doubt that I was the Nipple killer. They put out a picture of me, and my motorcycle, with and without my disguise. They asked anyone who sees me to immediately report it to the police. They said I could be armed and dangerous and might be wearing a disguise.

I drove around on my motorcycle and decided to hide it near El Paso. I walked around. I wanted to give the police a run for their money. I had to do something, and it had to be spectacular. I had the attention of the whole country. They were all looking for me. They knew it would not be easy.

I decided to go to El Paso, to a gated community, where the wealthy people lived. I looked around to see where the cameras were. I saw an air-conditioning repair man in a van that was about to turn into the complex. He was waiting for the light to change, when I entered the van. I pointed the gun at his head and ordered him to drive forward. We drove for a few minutes and asked him to stop. He had the order book open that showed the name, and the address of the house where he was going to repair the air conditioning unit. He had the company overalls on, that had the name of the company and logo, "Be Cool", and in front was his name, Walter. We drove into this empty field, we went to the back, where there were some trees. I had him take off his overalls. I took of my shirt and wrapped it around the gun so it would not make so much noise, and then I shot him in the head.

I quickly put the overalls on and drove back to the gated community. I went up to the security guard, told him I was Walter, with the company "be cool ", I was coming to repair the air condition unit for the Jones family. The guard got on the phone and inquired to see if they were expecting an air condition repair man from "Be Cool". They told him to let me in. The guard told me how to get to the house where they were expecting me.

When I arrived to the house, the lady was leaving, she told me where the air conditioning unit was. She told me she was going to work, and to repair it, and she would later pay the bill. She pulled out of the garage, and I went inside. I made myself a sandwich and turned on the TV. The whole country was looking for me. They had pictures of me without and with disguise, and possible other disguises. With sunglasses, with reading glasses. They had my weight, complexion, and height.

While I was in the house, I heard someone open the door. It was a teenage girl arriving home. She had her earphones on. She was moving to the music.

When I came down from the van, I had brought down Walter's toolbox so that the lady would think I really was the air condition man. In the box was a roll of duck type. The girl had no idea where I was. I am sure she saw the air condition repair van in the driveway.

I came up behind her and put my hand over her mouth. I told her not to make a sound. I pointed my gun at her head, then I placed some duct tape over her mouth, and wrapped it around her head. I hit her on the side of the head with my gun, and she passed out. I took her clothing off. I went into the kitchen; they had several knives in a wooden block on top of the counter. I took a knife and cut her throat. She began to bleed severely. I got a stiff erection, and I violently raped her. As usual, I began to shake violently. I was hyperventilating. I couldn't stand up. It finally passed.

Now I didn't have to hide the evidence. I wanted them to know I had been there; and I had done it.

I cut off her left nipple, then I got in the van. I had lots of blood on my overalls, but it was mostly below my waist. After washing off most of the blood, I took a towel from the bathroom, and placed it on top of my lap, so the guard could not see the blood, and he let me out. I drove back to my motorcycle, and dumped the van, and the overalls. I left the nipple on top of the dash in the van.

I took it as a challenge to avoid capture. I went on my motorcycle and dumped the bike an hour later. I walked a few miles and found a house that appeared abandoned. I looked through the windows, and looked around the house, no one was home, so I busted the door, and walked inside. There was dust on top of the table, and furniture. I could see that no one had been there for a while. I opened the refrigerator, and there was some stale bread, cheese, coca cola cans, beer, dried up apples and peaches. In the freezer, there was ground beef, chicken, ham, and ice-cream. In the kitchen wall was the keys hanging on a hook that appeared to be for the car on the driveway. On the shelf in the back room, in the entrance to the garage there was a shotgun, flashlights, and a machete. The garage had an old car and stored junk.

I turned on the TV. They had found the girl, and the blood all over the house. The police were desperate. The press showed the mother screaming with desperation. The girl was naked and had the left nipple gone. The press was all over the outside of the house. The police set up a perimeter and would not let anyone nearby. They were not sharing the details with the press.

Her father was an airline piolet and apparently had not been informed of the violence that had taken place in his home, until he got to the airport. They chose not to inform him while flying the plane. The police were at the airport to meet him and bring him home.

Suddenly there was a news alert. They had found the Van, but they did not share with the media about the nipple on the dash. It was such a horrific, and terrible murder, the different news stations were warning their viewers not to permit children, and to be cautious, that this might impact sensitive individuals. Of course they were not telling the public about the nipple. Most people, including the press did not know why they called me the nipple killer. I changed channels, but every station was reporting the news of the nipple killer. They told people to be cautious and be careful with strangers. The news was reporting what the police was telling them, of course they were not actually showing the blood, or the naked girl. They were, however, able to show the van.

Again, another news alert, they had found the air condition repair man Walter, shot through the head. I was laughing, thinking that they were not going to catch me. I went in the bathroom and took a long shower. I looked in the bedroom closet, and found some blue jeans and a tee shirt, and changed clothing. I turned the TV off and fell asleep on the couch.

The next day I woke up thinking of what other assault I could do. I had to keep the police looking for me. I wanted to have the news talking about the nipple killer again. I was famous, and I had to give them another show.

I went outside. It was eight in the morning. This time, I really wanted to do something that the world will always remember me by. As I was walking, I saw a group of kids waiting for the school bus. We were in a rural area. When the school bus arrived, I let the kids get on, and suddenly, before the driver closed the door, I got in the school bus. I closed the door and shot the driver. I took the school bus down this desert road, then in front of all the kids, I looked for the oldest girl with the best tits, I took my knife, and slit her throat, and in front of the kids I proceeded to rape her. Then I cut off her left nipple, and placed it on the driver's seat, then I opened the door, and all the kids ran out. I went out of the school bus and walked to the house where I had stayed the night before. No one had seen or heard the massacre that had taken place in front of these kids.

The kids ran home, and the police got involved right away. I turned the TV on, and it was all over the news. People were horrified. This had really gone over the top. The kids came home and told the parents all about it, and the public finely understood why they called me the nipple killer. The kids had told their parents that I had cut off her left nipple. The police flooded the area looking for me.

They started having police escorts with the buses. The FBI sent hundreds of their detectives. Police were volunteering from all over the country to see how they could help to find this man from hell. I knew it was only a matter of time before they would find me. I was right under their nose.

I stayed the night in the same house. I did not turn on any lights. I fell asleep on the couch again while watching the news.

They blocked the roads all around. They were looking for me with helicopters. The town was in panic; the chief of police was the killer. They moved my wife and children for their protection. They interrogated my wife to see if they could get information to find me. They sealed the Mexican border and placed agents everywhere to prevent me from getting into Mexico.

I woke up from my deep sleep and found a man that was pointing a shotgun at me. Soon the police arrived and took me into custody. To my misfortune, the owner of the house, who had been on vacation, had arrived and noticed that the door had been forced open. The owner of the house went back and got his shotgun while his wife called 911. The police arrived immediately and were able to take me into custody.

It was the end of the road for me. I decided to tell them everything in detail. I showed them where I had hidden my equipment. I showed them the fire pit. We went into my safety box, where I had hidden the nipples. I pleaded guilty, against my attorney's advice, and the judge condemned me to death.

Dr. Martha White had been assigned as my psychologist, with whom I had daily sessions. I was hard to penetrate. I didn't care. I was unkind to her. I didn't pay attention. It was a waste of time. When they came to get me, I didn't want to go, but it was obligatory. They threatened me. They said they would put me in the "hole", solitary confinement, if I didn't go.

She was gentle and made me feel like she was my only friend. Little by little I began to open up to her, and she made me understand the horrific things that I had done. I started to realize that because I had such a disgraceful childhood, it did not give me the right to kill people, as I thought it did. She helped me unload the hate that I carried in my subconscious towards my parents, especially my mother. I understood finely that it did not give me the right to kill. She made me see the anger and rage I carried in me towards women and how they became my enemy. I began to understand the violent shaking that would take place after I violently raped and killed my victims. It was the rage that I unloaded.

The Chaplin had also been a great influence. He had helped me get rid of the evil in me.

My victims became my enemy, and I emptied my rage, while I demanded pleasure. Little by little, I began to understand the great damage I had done to my victims and their families and the community that trusted me. I began to feel shame and realized I did not deserve to live. I wanted to die, so I would not continue to live with the shame, the disgrace, and the guilty feelings I was experiencing. I started to think that my birth had been a great mistake. An aberration. A pregnancy with the devil. All of my anger and rage disappeared, and was replaced with sadness, shame, and guilt.

My attorney had advised me to plead innocent, but I knew the jig was up.

They did DNA analysis of all the nipples and confirmed the identity of all of the victims. There was finally peace in Seco. My family was humiliated. They condemned the people in town that had hired me, after knowing my behavior during my childhood and adolescence.

I guess I wanted to get caught. I knew that I was leaving evidence behind. I was careless, and subconsciously, I guess I wanted to get caught. It was over. All these women paid for the sadness of my life. I thought if it felt good, I had the right to do this. It was in me. Someone had to pay for the hurt, the damage, the disgraceful and violent programing of my sad life.

Now I sit in death row, waiting for my time. I need to die. The evil wiring of my brain had come to an end, and now it is time to weed out this aberration of an evil mistaken life.

My psychologist called it, sexual rage. The person I was violently assaulting sexually became my enemy, or maybe my mother. I was there to take all the pleasure, mixed with my anger, and rage, that made me kill my sexual enemy. When I would see them fighting for their life, with great intensity, mixed with despair, and hopelessness, that gave me great satisfaction.

Back when I was the chief of police, and I would hear the detectives, the FBI, and all the agents assigned to catching the nipple serial killer talk, inside of me I was laughing. I would come by and ask them how things were going. Until they discovered who I was, then it did not matter anymore. I just wanted to kill and be famous. I didn't care. I wanted to do the evilest thing I could, before they finally caught me.

I was good to my family; I did not want them to go through what I went through. I loved my wife, and I showed it. I was good to my kids and neighbors too. I was a regular good guy. I guess, now that I understand it better, after years of therapy, I now realize how sick I was. My pleasure was all that mattered, and my pleasure was evil.

I guess you have to live through it to understand it. No one in their minds could capture the images I have in my head since I was a child. Eating rotten food sometime from trash cans. From my earliest memories, I really did not know who my parents were. The TV, was all to me. My room stunk, because I had not received proper training about toilet issues. Survival was my problem.

Now it's all gone. No more rage. I guess I thought it was my right. Now my heart is sad, but not because I have to die. I deserve to die, but I am deeply sad for all the sadness I caused. The evil is gone. My attorney tells me we have to appeal, to show the unfairness that brought this evil, hate, and rage towards women that was inside me. I ask them to please let me die. I have suffered enough. Every day that goes by my sorrow burns in shame. Every time I go before the judge, I ask him to let me die.

They keep litigating trying to find excuses for my actions. There are no excuses. I am evil. I was the enemy of the people. I will never find peace. Please let me die.

The judge is afraid of making the wrong decision. Usually, the people in death row want to make excuses to stay alive. So, they keep me here year after year, because they can't make up their minds what to do with me. I have asked the court to please let me die. I told them I can't keep living with all the guilt and shame and pain I feel inside.

They have finally given me a date for my execution. I will be executed in three months. I keep counting the days, and now it has come to my final day. They have asked me if I want to talk to the Chaplin. My psychologist told me that I must forgive myself first, and then I can ask forgiveness from God. I don't know if there is forgiveness for what I have done.

I asked if I could have one final meeting with my posologist Dr. White. She came to visit me the night before my execution. We both cried together. We both knelt while I confessed to God all the evil I had done. I then said, God, I know there is probably no forgiveness for what I have done, but I want you to know that with all my heart and soul, I repent for all the evil I have done. I know I don't deserve forgiveness, just allow me to have peace.

Dr. White gave me a big, long hug. She asked me if I wanted her to be present and give me some support. I told her I did not want her to see me die. I shared with her that they had told me I could have one final wish. My wish was that they please not let any of my family be present for my execution.

The final morning of my life is here. They took me into a room where they laid me down. There was a large glass wall on one side, I thought this might be where all the people I have hurt have come to see me die. I laid down on the gurney. They tied me down, and placed a needle into my left forearm, and the lights went out.

www.ingramcontent.com/pod-product-compliance
Lightning Source LLC
Chambersburg PA
CBHW040332020826
48978CB00013BC/1283